Katie comes out to me

Sitting in my bedroom on a Friday
night playing video games when my
white sister Katie barged into my
bedroom wearing a sexy little
black dress. I said hot date
Katie and she said no. I said why
are you dressed up then.

Katie said I want to go to a
lesbian club but I don't want to
go alone. I said why not, it's
just other babes there just like
you and no guys. She said you are
coming with me and I said no I'm
not, I'm not dancing by myself all
night.

I'll go to a regular club if I
want to dance by myself thank you
very much. Katie said you won't
be dancing by yourself; you will
be dancing with me. I said ok but
why are we going to a lesbian
club, we can go to a regular club.

Katie said because I'm bisexual.
I said really no way, I thought
that was just a Hollywood thing.
Katie said no I like penises and
vaginas equally. I said wow I
never saw that coming, does your
mom Katherine know about this.
Katie said I want to tell her but
I haven't found the courage to
tell her yet. I said ok but if I
go dancing with you, I might get
hard.

Katie said I've seen your big
black cock before, I said very
true but you haven't felt it
before, Katie said if you go to
the lesbian club with me, I'll let
you do anything you want to me.
My eyes grew wide and Katie
laughed out loud.

I said give me 15 minutes to get
ready. Katie said thank you so
much you won't regret it. I said
I hope not, Katie hugged me tight
and kissed me on the lips then

went to her bedroom to wait for me
to get ready.

I moisturized, put on some cologne
then put on my club attire. I was
ready to hit the lesbian club with
Katie. Even though I was going
with Katie, I was unsure what was
going to happen. I went to her
room; the door was open and Katie
was sitting on her bed. I said
I'm ready. She took my hand and
we rolled out to the club.

At the door, the lesbian at the
door told me this is a lesbian
club. I said I'm well aware of
that and Katie said I told him. I
had to drag him here so please let
us in before he runs away. The
lesbian laughed out loud then let
us in.

When we walked in, I was the only
guy there. Everyone was looking
at us. I told Katie this is a bad

idea and she said relax they are
just jealous that I'm bisexual and
they are not. I laughed out loud.

Katie said let's dance you big
dick stud. I said your dirty and
she said I'm your dirty little
slut tonight. Katie dragged me to
the dance floor and held me tight.
I could feel her pussy on my cock
and her big titties on my chest.

I thought oh god I'm going to get
hard and we just started. I
smiled as Katie started grinding
on my cock. I became hard in no
time flat. Katie whispered in my
ears that was fast. I said I told
you I was going to get hard.

Katie said oh yeah, you know how
to make your little slut wet. I
said your wet already. Katie said
oh yeah and I'm not wearing any
panties. I said oh yeah, my
little slut, she took my hand and

put it between her sweet white
thighs.

Katie said see for yourself. I
felt nothing but a wet pussy, so I
pushed my finger into her wet
vagina. I moaned oh Katie, I love
you and she said I love you too,
baby. Katie kissed me as I
fingered her pussy. I worked her
pussy over until I felt extra
lubrication and a vibration.

Katie took my hand and sucked her
juices off my finger. I said wow
Katie. Katie pulled me up against
the wall and turned around. She
put that big bootie on my hard
cock and I worked it over
properly.

I reached up to squeeze her big
fucking tits as Katie leaned back.
I worked her ass over really good
for a long time. Katie twerked
that big booty on my cock up and

down. Katie made me ejaculate into my pants. I told her that was hot baby thanks Katie.

She said your welcome, aren't you glad that you came now. I said oh yeah very happy. We held each other tight and kissed for a long time.

Our own little world was interrupted when this hot blonde goddess came up to us and ask if she could join in the fun. She said my name is Sarah and I'm bisexual. Katie said I'm bisexual too. Sarah kissed me passionately and then she kissed Katie passionately too.

Katie said nice to meet you Sarah and I said nice to meet you too Sarah. Katie said I'm his little slut and Sarah said I'll be his little slut too.

Sarah started dancing with Katie
and I started grinding on Sarah's
big ass. Katie and Sarah started
making out. I took the
opportunity to massage Sarah's big
titties.

Sarah turned around and told me
that she loves my big cock on her
ass but it will feel better on my
pussy. She kissed me and started
grinding on my hard cock. Katie
started grinding on Sarah's big
ass then massaged her big titties.

Sarah reached down and stroked my
cock. I reached down between her
sweet white thighs then higher to
her pussy. I felt her wet pussy
and no panties. I pushed my
finger deep and Sarah said make
your little slut come.

I sped up my fingering of her wet
pussy and Sarah moaned oh god yes,
she came hard creaming my finger

in her little pink slit. She took
it out and sucked all her cream
off of my middle finger. Katie
said do you want to come home with
us.

Sarah said oh yeah, I never turn
down big dick and pussy. I smiled
and took both of them by the hand.
We walk to the car. Sarah said I
was behind you two in line and I
watched you go at it before I
joined in the fun.

I said cool, Katie said he is my
black brother, so if you want to
bail you can right now if you
like. Sarah said its cool, I like
both of you and I want his big
dick in me too. Katie said me
too, I've seen his big dick a few
times but we haven't fucked yet.

Sarah said what self-control, I
would have already fucked him
after seeing it the first time.

We climbed into the car and Sarah
followed us home. We went quietly
to Katie's bedroom.

We all shed our clothes and Katie
jumped on the bed. Sarah dove
headfirst into Katie's pussy. She
started eating Katie's pussy and I
spread Sarah's sweet cheeks. I
licked and sucked on her clit for
a while. I stopped and slammed my
cock forcefully up her tight cunt.
Sarah moaned oh god your big as
shit. I held her sweet hips and
took her hard.

Katie slid down and they kissed as
I fucked the shit out of Sarah's
pussy. Sarah came like crazy then
said your turn Katie. She bent
over and I rammed my cock up her
cunt very hard. Katie said damn
so big but so good as I pumped her
full of black cock.

I fucked her deep and hard. Sarah
smacked her ass and said take it
you little slut. I fucked her
harder and harder until she gave
up the cream to my black bone.
Sarah said get on top of me. I
mounted her and started pumping
with my pleasure stick.

Sarah held me tight as I gave it
to her hard. It didn't take long
before she gave up the cream. We
kissed for a little bit then I
said your turn Katie. I mounted
her and took her tight little
pussy hard. She screamed as I
fucked the shit out of her. I
couldn't take it anymore so I
filled my little slut Katie with
my warm seed of pleasure.

I said damn that was fun thanks my
little sluts both said your
welcome, you big dick stud. I
smiled and laid between them
holding hands. We fell asleep and

I don't remember much after that
happened.

I heard someone come into the
room. It was Katherine, she said
good morning Katie, breakfast is
ready. She pulled off the covers
and saw me naked with Katie.
Katherine said I hope there is an
explanation for this.

Then I heard oh god that is a big
black penis. Sarah said oh yeah,
Katherine jumped and said three of
you, oh wow. Katie said I'm
bisexual and these two are my
lovers. Sarah said I'm Sarah,
nice to meet you. Katherine said
nice to meet you too.

Katherine said so let me get this
straight, his penis penetrated
both of you last night. Sarah and
Katie said yeah. Sarah said his
sperm is in both of us. I said I
thought I only came in Katie.

Sarah said don't you remember me
riding you when I woke you up
during the night and I was horny.

I said oh yeah, my sperm is in
Sarah too. Katie said we are his
two little sluts. I smiled and
Katherine said wow, I need to wrap
my head around this then left the
room. I said at least she knows
your bisexual. Sarah said
sometimes it's better to rip the
band aid off.

Katie said yeah, let's go eat, I'm
starving. Sarah said me too. We
all put on clothes and went down
to breakfast. Katherine served us
and there was quiet as we ate.
Katie said I'm sorry mom, I wanted
to tell you for a long time.
Katherine said its ok, I still
love you even if you are bisexual.

Katherine turned to me and said
how long have you known about

Katie. I said not long, I found
out last night before she dragged
me kicking and screaming to a
lesbian club. Katherine laughed
then said I guess that's where you
met Sarah. Sarah said correct, I
still haven't told my parents yet.
Katherine said I think they would
like to know their daughter is
bisexual.

Sarah said I'll think about it,
Katie said I'll hold your hands
while you tell them. Sarah said
really, I would love that a lot.
Katie kissed Sarah, I kissed Katie
and Sarah. Katherine said I
definitely have to get use to
that, I kissed Katherine so that
she didn't feel left out.

She giggled and Sarah said I have
to go before I start getting calls
from my mom and dad. We hugged
and kissed then she left. Katie
said so when are you going to tell

dad. Katherine said never and we
all started laughing.

A few weeks later, Katie was
visiting a friend of hers. It was
just Katherine and me at home on a
Saturday morning. I woke up early
and went to Katherine's room in my
boxers. She was still asleep, I
took my boxers off and sneaked
into her bed quietly.

I said good morning Katherine, are
you getting up today or are we
starving for breakfast. Katherine
said how about some cuddle time
honey. I said sure Katherine. I
spooned her with my hard cock and
kissed her neck.

Katherine was totally naked as I
felt my hard cock settle between
her amazing ass. Katherine took
my hand and put them on her big
titties. She moaned and said
isn't this much better than

breakfast. I said oh yeah
squeezing her melons.

Katherine said how about you get
on top of your white mommy and
give me a proper roman hug. I
said my pleasure, Katherine. I
mounted her and she spread her
sweet white thighs.

I felt the warmth of her vagina
and the thorough wetness of it.
Katherine held me tight and
wrapped her legs around me. I
kissed her neck and she kissed
mine too. I said this is the best
hug ever and she said I couldn't
agree more baby. We held each
other for a while until Katherine
said I want to be your little slut
too.

I said oh yeah now we talking.
Katherine said stick that big
black penis in my white vagina and
make us both feel wonderful. I

said oh yeah Katherine. I tried
to push my penis into Katherine's
vagina and it went nowhere.

Katherine said I'm very tight down
there, you are going to have to
force that big thing into my tight
little hole. I held her tight and
pushed a lot harder until I was
able to break into her tight
little cunt.

I entered Katherine balls deep and
she moaned touchdown baby, your
big penis is in my vagina. I
kissed Katherine and started
pumping my penis in and out of her
vagina. Katherine moaned oh god
honey your big penis feels so
wonderful in my vagina.

I said your vagina feels amazing
on my penis. I said I love you
Katherine, she said I love you my
sweet black boy. I gave it to
Katherine strong and she took it,

I know she was pleased when I
heard her moan yes right their
baby as she orgasmed all over my
penis. We held each other as she
came down from her orgasm high.

Katherine said I want you to
penetrate me doggie. I said oh
yeah, she got on all fours and I
penetrated her again deep. I
smacked her ass and she moaned. I
massaged her ass as I gave it to
her firmly. I massaged the hell
out of her vagina from behind. I
held her hips and took her to
heaven. She willingly creamed my
penis yet again. Katherine said
how about I ride you until you
ejaculate into my vagina. I said
oh yeah, I love that idea.

I laid down as Katherine mounted
me holding my hard penis. She
slid her tight little vagina down
my lubricated pole. I squeezed
her melons as she slid up and down
my penis smiling with pleasure.

I moaned oh Katherine, you're so
good to me you little slut.
Katherine moaned I love being your
little slut for pleasure. She
rode me harder and I felt a great
pleasure before I exploded inside
of Katherine. I moaned oh
Katherine, I love you and she said
I love you too my stud.

Katherine leaned down and kissed
me. We held each other and kissed
for a long time. When we came up
for air, Katherine said I better
make breakfast, I'm starving and I
said me too. Katherine said
making love is quite tiring my
love.

Katherine dismounted my cock. I
watched her sexy ass jiggle to the
bathroom to get a robe. I watched
her smiling. When she left, I
laid in bed for a little bit, I
put on my boxers and went
downstairs.

I watched her make breakfast as we
couldn't stop smiling at each
other with lust, love and passion
all intertwined. When she
finished making us breakfast. We
sat down and ate looking at each
other longingly.

I said thanks for breakfast
Katherine. She said your welcome
honey. Later we were on the couch
cuddling when Katie came back. We
separated when we heard her close
the door. She said hey guys I'm
home. I said welcome back as we
were hugging and kissing each
other.

Months into our relationship with
Sarah. She asked us to come with
her to see her mom. Katie and I
knew what it was about, she was
going to come out to her mom with
both of us there. Katherine
wished us luck when we left.

When we arrived at her mom's place. Her mom Shannon opened the door. Sarah said these are two of my friends. Shannon welcomed us with open arms and told us to come on in. We went into her house and sat down. Sarah said there is something that I want to tell you mother.

Sarah said in case you down know; I am a bisexual woman and these are my two lovers. Shannon put her hand over her mouth and said wow, I didn't see that coming at all. Sarah said I'm sorry if this disappoints you mother.

Shannon said I'm not disappointed baby. I love you very much and thanks for telling me. I said that went better than I thought. Katie said oh yeah. Shannon said you lucky man, you get to please two white vaginas. I said oh yeah, I am very lucky.

Shannon said I bet you have a big
penis, I heard black men have big
penises, is that true. I said I
do have a big penis. Katie said
yeah, he has big penis and Sarah
said I love his big penis, it
gives us many orgasms. Shannon
said I bet and we all laugh out
loud.

Sarah said where is dad, Shannon
said on travel for work. Sarah
said should I tell him that I'm
bisexual. Shannon said oh hell
no, we won't be telling him about
this ever. Sarah said why not
mom, and Shannon said because he
is a religious nut and will get
upset.

I said oh boy, I'm glad he isn't
here today. Shannon said you and
me both, big daddy. Katie laughed
out loud. We all heard footsteps
then a woman's voice saying what's
taking so long Shannon. Then we
saw a woman with a strap on

totally naked walk out. Sarah
said oh my god mom, no wonder I'm
bisexual. Then Sarah said
Stefanie, I said what the hell,
you know her. Sarah said yeah,
it's my friend from high school
and she is doing your mother.

Shannon said I know this looks bad
but please don't tell your father
about this please. Sarah said
don't worry mom its ok. Stefanie
walked over and hugged Sarah, it's
so good to see you. Stefanie said
sorry about the strap on. Sarah
said its ok, this is my girlfriend
Katie and my boyfriend. We both
said nice to meet you that's when
she undid her strap on and it fell
to the ground.

I saw her pussy and I became hard
as a rock. Shannon saw my tent
and said wow that's big. Stefanie
said Sarah and Katie, you are both
lucky women. They both looked at
my pants and smiled then said yes,

we are very happy, the three of
us.

Sarah got up and sat on my lap
then said don't even think about
it, I know both of you are
bisexual. Shannon said this is
true and Stefanie said very true.

Stefanie said I better go put on a
robe like your mother is wearing.
She left and came back. We all
sat around talking and looking at
each other smiling until it was
time to leave.

There was a lot of long hugs and
kisses before we left. Sarah had
to pull her mom Shannon and
Stefanie off of me so that we
could leave with my boner still in
my pants.

We were walking to the car and I
said wow that was more fun that I

thought it was going to be. Katie
said oh yeah, I'll never forget
this as long as I shall live.

Sarah dropped us off then went
home. We told Katherine all about
our trip, her eyes almost popped
out of her head and she laughed a
lot.

A month later, Sarah was spending
the night over at our house.
Katie, Sarah and I were asleep. I
felt a hand on my cock, I thought
it was Sarah or Katie. When I
opened my eyes it was Katherine,
she whispered sorry honey I miss
and need your big dick in me.

She held my pole at full attention
and slid her tight pink vagina
down my pleasure pole. Damn it
felt good to be inside Katherine
with her daughter Katie and Sarah
right there.

Katherine slowly fucked my cock as
I squeezed her big breasts. She
bit her lips so that she didn't
make noise. Katherine rode me
fast and I squeezed her juicy ass.
She moaned out loud but Sarah and
Katie remained asleep.

Katherine fucked me harder and
that woke up Katie and Sarah.
Katie said oh my god you slut, you
are fucking our boyfriend. Sarah
said oh my god she is his third
slut and Katie laughed. Katherine
kept fucking me harder and said
I'm sorry ladies but his big penis
is hard for me to resist.

Sarah said this is so hot your
mother fucking her black son and
our boyfriend looking at Katie.
Sarah then surprised us by French
kissing Katherine with no
resistance whatsoever. I looked
at Katie and moaned oh god I'm
coming in your hot mom. Katie

smiled then French kissed me
passionately.

The end

www.ingramcontent.com/pod-product-compliance
Lightning Source LLC
Chambersburg PA
CBHW070735160726
48003CB00006BA/2528